P9-DYE-109

It's Ancient History!

Adapted by Ellie O'Ryan
Based on the series created by Dan Povenmire & Jeff "Swampy" Marsh

DISNEP PRESS
New York

Copyright © 2011 Disney Enterprises, Inc.

All rights reserved. Published by Disney Press, an imprint of Disney Book Group. No part of this book may be reproduced or transmitted in any form or by any means, electronic or mechanical, including photocopying, recording, or by any information storage and retrieval system, without written permission from the publisher. For information address Disney Press, 114 Fifth Avenue, New York, New York 10011-5690.

Printed in the United States of America
First Edition
10 9 8 7 6 5 4 3 2 1
J689-1817-1-10305

Library of Congress Catalog Card Number on file.
ISBN 978-1-4231-2742-0

For more Disney Press fun, visit www.disneybooks.com
Visit DisneyChannel.com

If you purchased this book without a cover, you should be aware that this book is stolen property. It was reported as "unsold and destroyed" to the publisher, and neither the author nor the publisher has received any payment for this "stripped" book.

Part One

Chapter 1

It was another beautiful summer day in Danville, but Phineas Flynn and Ferb Fletcher weren't outside enjoying the sunshine. That's because the stepbrothers had decided to spend the morning in the cool, marble confines of the Danville Museum. The museum was crowded with people who were checking out a new exhibit of Greek artifacts. Phineas and Ferb were so excited about it they had brought

their parents, their sister, Candace Flynn, and even their pet platypus, Perry, to the museum.

Unlike Phineas and Ferb, though, Candace wasn't a bit interested in the exhibit. "I can't believe you guys dragged me all the way over here for *this*," she complained, rolling her eyes as she looked at the ancient statues.

"Guys! Come and look at this!" Mr. Fletcher, their father, called excitedly. His British accent boomed through the quiet hallways of the museum. "This is an actual replica of an artist's interpretation of what some random guy of no significance believed

4

the Chariot of Asparagus might have looked like!" Mr. Fletcher was clearly impressed.

Phineas and Ferb joined their dad, who was pointing to an ivory chariot with shiny gold trim. "And this is Asparagus, the greatest warrior in all of Greece," Mr. Fletcher continued as he pointed to an oil painting on the wall. "With his golden chariot, he would win every race! And here he is defeating the Minotaur, a creature that's half-man, half-bull. Asparagus defeated him using the head of Medusa, a

creature so ugly she could turn people to stone with just one look."

Phineas and Ferb stood back to admire the marble statue of Medusa. The statue's face was twisted in an ugly snarl. Instead of hair, there were angry snakes wrapped around her head. Phineas thought Medusa looked like an awesome monster!

"Kind of reminds me of Candace," he joked.

But Candace didn't think Phineas was funny at all. "It does *not* look like me!" she yelled, putting her hands in the air—and looking even more like the scary statue!

Suddenly Phineas had an idea. "I know what we're going to do today!" he told Ferb. "We're going to have our own chariot race!"

While Ferb grinned back at Phineas, Candace narrowed her eyes and frowned. Ever since her mom had married Mr. Fletcher and Ferb had officially become her stepbrother, Candace had been constantly annoyed by him and Phineas. They did one crazy thing after another—and they *never* got in trouble! Phineas and Ferb were thrilled when their parents got married, though. They felt more like real brothers than stepbrothers—and even better, they were best friends, too!

But just because Candace hadn't been able to bust Phineas and Ferb before didn't mean she was going to stop trying. Phineas's chariot race sounded like the perfect opportunity to catch her brothers doing something crazy.

And this time, Candace was going to make sure that her parents found out about it!

As soon as they got home, Phineas and Ferb dusted off their scale model of the city of Danville so they could plan a course for the chariot race. "Okay," Phineas began, tapping a pointer on the miniature city streets as he spoke. "The race will start here at home, then head through the streets of Danville and over to the park. From there we make our way past Paul Bunyan's Pancake Haus and finish at the steps of the museum."

Before Ferb could comment, Mr. Fletcher walked up to the boys carrying a tall stack of

videotapes. He was wearing a bronze helmet, complete with a fluffy red plume. He looked just like someone from ancient times. "Hey, boys," their dad said. "What are you doing?"

"Just mapping out our route for the big chariot race we're going to have," Phineas replied.

"Oh, excellent!" Mr. Fletcher exclaimed. As he glanced at the model of Danville and the tiny horse-and-chariot figurines, Mr. Fletcher assumed that Phineas and Ferb were just playing a game. But he couldn't have been more wrong!

"Well, it's good to see you boys taking an interest in Greek mythology," Mr. Fletcher continued. "I'm doing the same. I've got over twelve hours of gladiator movies here that I want to watch."

Just then, Phineas and Ferb's friend Isabella Garcia-Shapiro joined the group. "Nice hat, Mr. Fletcher!" she called out.

"Thank you, Isabella!" Mr. Fletcher replied, tapping his helmet. "It's my movie-watching hat!" He smiled at the kids, then hurried inside to start his gladiator-movie marathon.

"Isabella, we're going to have the greatest race in history, complete with helmets and armor and supercool chariots with horses!" Phineas exclaimed. "Spread the word! Spread the word!"

Isabella nodded enthusiastically and ran off to tell everyone she knew. Suddenly, she stopped and ran back to Phineas and Ferb. "Wait. At what time?" she asked.

"In about an hour or so," Phineas told her.

Isabella gave Phineas a thumbs-up and

hurried away—only to stop and run back again. "Where's it going to be?" she asked.

"Here!" Phineas replied excitedly.

Once more, Isabella raced off to announce the chariot race—when one more question stopped her. "Who am I telling again?" she called out.

"Just spread the word!" Phineas yelled back. "Oh, and tell them to bring gladiator gear!" Phineas knew that one thing was certain about a modern-day chariot race: wearing the right gladiator gear would be essential. He had a feeling it was going to be a bumpy ride!

Chapter 2

Phineas and Ferb had been so excited about planning the chariot race that they hadn't noticed that their pet platypus, Perry, stayed behind at the museum. That was exactly what Perry had wanted. Because Perry was not just an adorable pet—he was also a top secret operative known by the code name Agent P! He was an expert at sneaking off to complete various missions.

As Perry crept through the museum, he suddenly heard someone whispering.

"Psst! Agent P! Over here!" the voice said.

Perry slapped a fedora onto his head, instantly transforming himself into Agent P. He hid behind a Grecian urn that was next to an enormous statue of a discus player. The statue must have

been hollow, though, because Major Monogram—Perry's superior officer and the commander of the agency—was hiding inside it!

"Sorry to disturb you here at the museum," Major Monogram continued in a hushed voice. "We've just been informed that Dr. Doofenshmirtz has created a machine to rid the world of platypuses." Major Monogram gave Perry a serious look. "We've tracked him

to the old abandoned movie house. So get going!" he finished.

Agent P nodded. Dr. Doofenshmirtz was his enemy, and it was no secret that the evil doctor was angry with Agent P for always spoiling his evil plots. But Perry had never imagined that Dr. Doofenshmirtz would try to permanently eliminate Perry's whole species!

Agent P straightened his hat. He had a very serious plot to foil—and there wasn't a moment to lose!

Agent P raced to the old movie theater, which had recently been renamed Doofenshmirtz Abandoned Theater. It was clear why no one else wanted it: the floor was sticky with spilled soda; the seats were covered with chewed-up bubble gum; and the projector was so old that it made a *clack-clackety-clack* noise during movies—when it actually worked, that is. Slowly, Agent P crept down the aisle, carrying a bucket of popcorn so that he would look like a regular moviegoer. In reality, though, Agent P was looking out for Dr. Doofenshmirtz as he tiptoed around the empty soda cups and popcorn containers that had been thrown on the floor.

There was no sign of Dr. Doofenshmirtz anywhere, but Agent P didn't let down his guard. He slipped into a seat and waited patiently for the evil doctor to appear.

But suddenly, without any warning, two metal clamps sprang out of the armrests— and handcuffed Agent P to the seat!

"Comfy, Perry the Platypus?" a voice cackled gleefully.

It was Dr. Doofenshmirtz! Agent P had walked right into a trap!

The doctor passed in front of the screen. He grinned as he shoved his hands into the pockets of his white lab coat. "I've prepared something special just for you!" Dr. Doofenshmirtz declared. "You see, until now, every attempt to eradicate you has been foiled. Then I came across some—"

Ssssslurp. Ssssslurp. S-s-s-s-s-s-slurp!

Dr. Doofenshmirtz frowned at this rude interruption of his speech. He looked around and noticed a bored-looking teenager sitting nearby, loudly slurping a soda.

"Excuse me?" Dr. Doofenshmirtz asked. "Who are you, and what are you *doing* here?"

"I bought a ticket to see this movie," the boy replied casually.

Dr. Doofenshmirtz examined the ticket and sighed. The teenager had every right to be there—even if the kid *was* ruining the sinister atmosphere Dr. Doofenshmirtz had worked so hard to create. "Okay, just roll the film," Dr. Doofenshmirtz said as he slumped into the seat next to Agent P.

The ancient projector came to life as an old documentary appeared on the screen. "Who is the enemy of the platypuses?" the narrator asked in a serious voice.

As the film played, Dr. Doofenshmirtz gave Agent P some of his popcorn. Just because they were sworn enemies didn't mean they couldn't enjoy a tasty snack together!

"The platypus is one of our greatest friends in nature," the narrator continued. "A humble but key component in Mother Nature's delicate cycle of life." A grid flashed across the

screen, showing how the platypus was connected to all sorts of different creatures, from spiders and turkeys to elephants and even people.

"But as of late, worldwide populations have been declining to near endangerment," the narrator informed the audience, as one by one, platypuses disappeared from the screen! "But why? Who is the enemy of the platypuses?"

Agent P, Dr. Doofenshmirtz, and the random teenager stared at the screen, completely captivated by the film. "This is the best platypus movie I have ever seen!" the teenager exclaimed as he took another loud sip of his soda and helped himself to a handful of popcorn.

"Historically, the enemies of the platypus were well-known," the narrator continued.

"But there is a new enemy of the platypus," he reported. "One whose tireless development paves over the platypuses' woodland homes."

The movie zoomed in on a neighborhood filled with row after row of houses.

"The greatest enemy of the platypus . . . is man!" the narrator announced as a figure of a human appeared onscreen.

Dr. Doofenshmirtz's eyes lit up as he threw his popcorn to the side. "Ah! You see, Perry the Platypus, for *years* I've been trying to rid myself of you with traps and bombs and poisonous gases and automatic tennis-ball machines . . . I don't even know what I was thinking back then!" he cried. "But now I have the *ultimate* platypus-elimination weapon!"

Dr. Doofenshmirtz leaped to his feet and pulled a remote control out of his pocket. "Perry the Platypus, recoil in horror at my new creation: a giant . . . killer . . . robot . . . *man!*" he shrieked.

As Dr. Doofenshmirtz laughed evilly, he pressed a button on the remote control. From a shadowy corner of the movie theater, an enormous figure approached. The sound of clanging metal filled the theater. When the creature stood in front of the flickering projection light, Agent P could finally see what it was: an enormous metallic robot, wearing a suit and tie!

"My name is Norm!" The robot's booming voice filled the theater. He reached out to shake Perry's hand as he introduced himself. Agent P frowned. *This* was the big threat? He had already met Norm during a previous mission to try and stop Dr. Doofenshmirtz. Norm was a pretty friendly robot.

Just then, Norm's eyeball sensors focused on Agent P. His computerized brain started to send a message: TARGET IDENTIFIED! TARGET IDENTIFIED! In seconds, a blinking target focused on Agent P. "The enemy of the platypus is man!" Norm announced.

In a flash of metal, Norm's gigantic hand smashed down on Agent P's seat—but Perry was ready for him. He slipped out of his handcuffs and jumped out of the way just in time to escape Norm's powerful fist. The seat, though,

was not so lucky. It split into hundreds of tiny pieces! Agent P frowned. Maybe Norm wasn't so friendly after all!

"This is awesome!" exclaimed the teenager, who had been watching the entire thing. "I didn't know this movie was in 3-D!" He slurped his soda again.

At that moment, Agent P leaped over the boy, then zoomed down the aisle toward the theater exit as he tried to escape from Norm.

"Please, stop running," Norm requested politely. *Clang! Clang! Clang!* The floor shook as Norm took several giant steps toward Agent P.

"Perhaps we could discuss our differences

over coffee?" Norm suggested as he crashed through the wall.

But Perry just ran faster. Norm seemed determined to catch him, and Agent P wasn't going to take any chances.

Chapter 3

After much preparation, Phineas and Ferb were finally ready for the big chariot race! They'd built dozens of tall columns that towered over their yard. They had also constructed a platform to hold an Olympic-style flame that flickered in the warm summer breeze. An enormous banner stretched between two pillars, proclaiming CHARIOT RACE! in Greek-style letters.

"Okay, we're all set!" Phineas announced as kids entered the backyard. He buckled a bronze helmet with an impressive red plume, fastening it under his chin. "Let's meet our racers!"

Phineas strolled over to the first chariot. Ferb was standing next to it, wearing a matching helmet. Their chariot was red with gold stripes and purple trim. "In the first chariot is us," Phineas said. "Then we've got Isabella and the Fireside Girls."

Isabella and two of her friends waved to the

crowd. All three girls wore bronze helmets and armor as they stood next to their orange-and-gold chariot.

Phineas gestured toward the other two racers. "Buford and Baljeet," he said, introducing two of his his other friends. Like the rest of the racers, Buford Van Stomm and Baljeet Patel wore helmets. Baljeet's bronze helmet had a sharp, pointy ridge coming out of the top, while Buford's steel helmet had a pair of decorative wings sticking out from it. Their brown chariot had wings as well.

"And we have a chariot for Candace, too, if

she ever shows up," Phineas finished. "Here are the maps for everyone. The first chariot to reach the museum wins! Any questions?"

"Um, yes," Baljeet replied, waving his hand in the air. "Should we not establish the rules first?"

"This is a chariot race!" Buford shouted. "There are no rules!"

"No rules?!" Isabella gasped. Her eyes grew wide. Then she shrugged. "Well, if those are the rules . . ."

Buford leaned over Baljeet and poked him

in the chest. "Hey, you!" Buford snarled. "You're going down!"

"But we are on the same team!" Baljeet protested.

"Then you're going down with me!" Buford growled back.

"Each chariot will be pulled by a rocking horse that Ferb souped-up with a lawn-mower engine," Phineas explained. He showed the group how to control their vehicles.

Suddenly, a shrill voice interrupted Phineas's

instructions. "Phineas!" Candace yelled. "Just *what* do you think you're doing?"

"Candace, great!" Phineas exclaimed. "You're right on time. Check out this cool-looking helmet we made for you!"

Phineas smiled and handed Candace a gleaming helmet that was decorated with dozens of bronze snakes. It looked strangely like the Medusa statue they had seen in the museum. Candace eyed it suspiciously.

"And we built you your own chariot that looks just like you," Phineas continued. He pointed toward a terrifying-looking chariot. It had a woman's face painted on it, with a giant, snarling mouth and even more snakes twisting out of her head!

"Oh, that's ridiculous," Candace said, making a face that looked identical to the one painted on the chariot. "I do *not* have wheels!"

Candace spun around and marched into

the house. She found her dad sitting on the couch, munching on some popcorn as he watched his gladiator-movie marathon. Perfect! She was going to bust her brothers this time!

"Dad, they're racing chariots!" Candace announced, ready for her father to jump up and join her outside.

"Yes! The scene's just starting," Mr. Fletcher replied, his eyes glued to the screen. "Come in and sit down."

Candace glanced out the window, where

she saw Phineas and Ferb climbing into their chariot. "Come on, Candace!" Phineas shouted as he waved to her. The race was about to begin, and he didn't want his sister to get a late start.

"*Dad!*" Candace shrieked. She suddenly realized that if Mr. Fletcher didn't get up now—*right* now—Phineas and Ferb would zoom off . . . and get away with another one of their crazy ideas!

"Oh, I'm sorry," Mr. Fletcher replied, offering the bowl of popcorn to Candace. "Do you want some?"

"That's it!" Candace shouted. "I'll stop this myself!"

Outside, the kids revved their lawn-mower engines and rolled their chariots up to the starting line.

Another one of the boys' friends, Django Brown, began to count down to the start of the race. He was wearing a toga made out of a

bedsheet. "At your ready . . . get set . . . *go!*" Django yelled loudly.

The chariots zoomed off, with a crowd of kids chasing behind them. Just then, Candace stormed outside. "Okay, you two, I've had enough of this— Ow! Hey!" she cried.

In all the commotion at the start of the race, the bronze helmet Phineas had made for Candace flew through the air and landed firmly on her head. Candace stumbled around as she tried to take it off. Then she accidentally knocked into one of the massive columns the boys had built! One by one, the others toppled like a set of gigantic dominoes. Candace jumped out of the way of the pillars

just in time, but as she did, her chariot's safety harness got looped around her foot. The lawn-mower engine suddenly roared to life, and the chariot sped off—dragging Candace behind it!

"*Ahhhhhhhhhhh!*" Candace screamed as she flipped into the runaway chariot. Now she was in the driver's seat!

The sound of Candace screaming finally captured Mr. Fletcher's attention. He turned around to glance out the window. But he was just a moment too late; Candace and the out-of-control chariot had disappeared. "Oh, now where'd she go?" Mr. Fletcher wondered out loud. "She's going to miss all the excitement!"

But Mr. Fletcher couldn't have been more wrong—Candace was about to have the ride of her life!

Chapter 4

The four chariots zoomed down the streets of Danville at top speed. Each charioteer was determined to take the lead—except for Candace. She was terrified!

Buford's eyes narrowed as Phineas and Ferb raced into first place. Then he revved his engine and a nasty smile crossed his face. Buford edged his chariot closer and closer to them. Just then, sharp spikes popped out from

the wheels of Buford's vehicle and stabbed the wheels of Phineas and Ferb's chariot!

Phineas frowned as he glanced down at the tires. Luckily, they hadn't suffered any damage—yet. "Remind me, why did we put spikes on Buford's chariot?" Phineas asked Ferb. Ferb just shrugged. Spikes had seemed

like a perfect addition to the vehicle . . . but that was *before* Buford decided to actually use them!

Buford cackled as he and Baljeet pulled into the lead. But that just made Phineas and Ferb more determined to win! The stepbrothers held on tight as their chariot sped up.

Meanwhile, Candace finally got her chariot under control. And now that she wasn't so terrified, she had a chance to figure out all of the laws that Phineas and Ferb were actually breaking. "Reckless endangerment, disrupting traffic—oh, they are *so* busted!" Candace exclaimed. She took out her cell phone to call her parents.

But Phineas and Ferb had bigger problems to deal with—like the fact that Buford was about to launch a bowling ball at them!

Whoooosh!

Phineas and Ferb ducked into their chariot as the bowling ball sailed over their heads.

"A bowling-ball catapult?" Phineas asked. "I mean, what were we thinking?"

The ball hit the pavement and bounced back into the air. It knocked Candace's cell phone right out of her hand.

"My phone!" Candace gasped as her cell phone clattered onto the street. Now she wouldn't be able to call either of her parents to tell them what was going on. Candace would have to bust Phineas and Ferb herself!

Suddenly, Buford and Baljeet took the lead once more! "Why'd you give *them* all the cool stuff?" Phineas asked Ferb, frowning. "What do we have?"

Ferb pressed a button on the chariot's dashboard. Immediately, an automated cup holder appeared, presenting two ice-cold drinks.

"Cup holders? Sweet!" Phineas cheered. "Now we're cooking!"

While Buford and Baljeet battled Phineas and Ferb to remain in first place, Isabella and her team inched ahead. If they kept up their momentum, the girls would have a good chance at taking the lead!

"The girls are still gaining on us," Baljeet

told Buford nervously. "Failure is not an option for me, my friend!"

"Well, use your head and think of something, genius!" Buford shot back.

Baljeet was suddenly inspired by Buford's remark. "Exactly!" he cried. "Use my head!" Following Baljeet's "instructions," Buford tipped Baljeet over the side of the chariot. Buford carefully lowered Baljeet until the razor-sharp edge of his helmet just barely touched the ground. The friction of the bronze helmet against the hard pavement sent sparks flying through the air—right toward Isabella's chariot!

"That's right! Eat sparks, my opponents!"

Baljeet cried as the top of his helmet banged along the street.

Phineas sniffed at the air. "Do you smell something burning?" he asked Ferb.

Isabella and her teammates ducked into their chariot to hide from the fiery sparks. Within moments, they fell behind the other chariots and were soon in last place.

"An unconventional way to use my head, yes," Baljeet commented, "but an effective one!"

At that moment, Agent P sprinted down an alley that crossed the chariot race, with Norm the robot in pursuit! Just when Agent P thought he had escaped from the dangerous robot, he dared to peek over his shoulder . . . only to discover that Norm was just a few feet behind him!

"We should do this more often," Norm said, smiling at Agent P.

WHAM! Norm's clenched fist smashed into the pavement, creating a giant pothole—and narrowly missing Agent P!

As he leaped out of Norm's way, Perry barely had time to notice the four chariots thundering down the street at top speed. Isabella and her friends were ready to fight back against Buford and Baljeet. With perfect aim, Isabella lassoed a strong rope around a streetlight.

"Okay, girls," Isabella called to her team. "Star formation!"

The Fireside Girls knew exactly what to do. Linking hands and stretching out their arms, they formed a perfect star across the chariot. Isabella leaned out one side, holding a hook that was attached to the other end of the rope. As the chariot sped up, Isabella took a deep breath. She would have only one chance to take the lead from Buford and Baljeet.

In seconds, the girls' chariot had reached Buford and Baljeet's vehicle. The boys could only watch in shock as Isabella snagged the hook on their chariot. Then Buford and Baljeet's chariot was flung all the way back to the streetlight!

"Sorry! No rules!" Isabella reminded them. Her chariot sped into first place.

Buford and Baljeet frowned at the thick rope that bound their vehicle to the streetlight.

"Now what?" Baljeet asked.

"You'll have to use your head again," Buford growled. Before Baljeet could reply, he grabbed him by the ankles and swung him toward the rope. The sharp edge on Baljeet's helmet instantly sliced through it, and the boys' chariot was free! As it zoomed down the

sidewalk, Buford was so focused on gaining the lead that he started driving very recklessly. The boys' chariot bumped into Candace's vehicle, accidentally knocking Candace right into Buford's lap!

"Hey!" Buford snarled at her. "Get back on your own chariot!" Buford launched Candace back toward her racer, but she landed on the wooden horse in front of the vehicle instead of in the cart. All Candace could do now was hold on tight!

The four chariots careened into Danville Park. The kids yanked on the reins with all

their might as they swerved quickly around the trees—except for Buford. Buford just swung Baljeet back and forth so that Baljeet's sharp-edged helmet would cut down each and every tree in their path! But Buford's newfound lumberjack skills did nothing to make the course easier for Candace. Now she had to dodge flying tree trunks, too! As the four chariots zoomed out of the park, Candace held on tightly to the front of the chariot. She couldn't believe the extreme danger she was in—and it was all thanks to Phineas and Ferb!

Chapter 5

Phineas grabbed a map so he could figure out where they were. "We should be coming up on Paul Bunyan's Pancake Haus," he yelled to Ferb.

Seconds later, the restaurant appeared on the left. Towering statues of Paul Bunyan and his big blue ox told Phineas that they were on the right track. "Oh, there it is!" Phineas exclaimed.

As Phineas and Ferb zipped past the pancake house, a new duo raced up behind them. It was Agent P and Norm!

"Are those slacks new?" Norm bellowed happily. "They make you look slimmer!"

But Agent P wasn't fooled by Norm's compliments. He knew that the robot had been programmed for one task and one task only: platypus elimination! Perry took advantage of being smaller than Norm to confuse the robot with some fancy footwork. Norm staggered around, trying to stomp on Agent P. Instead, the giant robot crashed right into the statue of Paul Bunyan's ox! The force of the crash broke the head off the ox statue. It spun through the air and landed right on Norm's enormous head!

Perry knew that now might be his only chance to escape from Norm. He dashed into the street—and nearly collided with Phineas and Ferb's chariot! Agent P instantly tossed off

his hat to transform back into Perry the Platypus.

"Look, it's Perry!" Phineas exclaimed. He reached down to scoop up his pet. "Where've you been?"

Clang! Clang! Clang!

A thundering crash made Phineas look up.

His eyes widened. "What is *that*?" he asked in amazement.

Norm, still wearing the ox head, was stumbling after them!

"It's half-man, half-bull!" Phineas gasped. "It's the Minotaur!"

"My name is Norm!" the robot announced.

"It's *Norm* the Minotaur!" exclaimed Phineas. "Hit it, Ferb!"

Ferb snapped the reins as the robot focused his attention back on Perry. Even when wearing an ox head, Norm was still programmed to destroy any platypus in the area.

"Wait! Come back!" Norm begged Phineas and Ferb. "You can borrow my rake!"

Just like Perry, Phineas and Ferb weren't about to be tricked by Norm's politeness. They wanted to get far away from the gigantic robot—as quickly as possible!

Meanwhile, Candace's crazy chariot ride had gone from bad to worse. Since she didn't know how to steer the vehicle, Candace was powerless to stop it from zooming through a car wash. When the chariot came out, it was sparkling clean—but Candace was soaked and covered in bubbles!

Then the chariot slammed into a giant fruit-and-vegetable stand, leaving Candace with a pineapple in her mouth and fruit salad on her head! But that was nothing compared to what happened next. Candace's vehicle crashed through a fish stand—and dozens of slimy, stinky fish slapped her across the face. Candace groaned. She started to wish for another spin through the car wash.

But there was one upside to Candace's wild ride: her speeding chariot lurched into first place!

"Candace has the lead!" Phineas cheered. "Go, Candace!"

"Somebody *help* me!" Candace screamed.

"See, I knew she'd love it," Phineas said with a big grin on his face.

The four chariots raced up the steps of the Danville Museum. The chariot race's big finish was just moments away! But Norm was still stampeding after them. The ox head hadn't slowed him down at all.

Crowds of kids gathered on either side of the museum's entrance. They held their

breath as they waited to see who would be crowned the champion.

"Candace wins!" Django announced as she crossed the finish line. He jumped up and down, causing the olive branches he was wearing behind his ears to almost fall off.

But the chariots were going too fast to stop! They zoomed into the museum and crashed into the ancient Greek artifacts exhibit! Marble statues shattered and the four chariots scattered everywhere in a cloud of smoke and dust.

Once the dust had settled, Phineas turned and smiled. "That was the coolest rocking-horse, mower-pulled chariot, Minotaur chase

49

ever!" he exclaimed as he and Ferb dusted themselves off in front of an ancient Greek platypus display.

"Gross," Candace complained as she struggled to climb out of a stuffed lion. Despite the crash, the snake-covered helmet was still firmly stuck on her head.

"Phineas! And Ferb! Phineas! And Ferb!" cheered the crowd. What an exciting race!

The cheers for her brothers only made Candace angrier. "Oh, *no,*" she yelled as she stormed up to them. "No, no, no, no, *no!* You *can't* just tear up the town with your chariots and expect to get away with it. When Mom and Dad find out about this—"

Clang! Clang! Clang!

Candace was suddenly interrupted when Norm marched into the museum. The giant robot was setting his target on the platypus exhibit right behind Phineas and Ferb!

"Candace," Phineas interrupted, trying to warn his sister about Norm.

"The enemy of the platypus is man," Norm announced.

Candace spun around to see what was behind her. "Listen, pal, you stay out of this!" she shouted at Norm.

Just then, Agent P swung through the museum on a rope. As he passed Norm's back, he flipped the robot's power switch to OFF. Then he swung off to safety, completely unnoticed by the crowd. The enormous robot swayed back and forth for a moment. Then Norm crashed to the floor!

The crowd gathered around the motionless robot and just stared at it in shock.

"She turned him to stone!" Django yelled, pointing at Candace.

"I did *what?*" Candace asked, confused. As the lights from the museum made the snakes on her helmet shine, the kids began to scream and run away.

"Don't look at her! It's Medusa!" one girl shrieked. Even Ferb covered his eyes.

"Wait!" Candace cried. But it was no use.

Everyone was terrified of her. "Oh, that's it. I'm out of here!"

"Wait! Candace!" Phineas called, running after her.

At that moment, Dr. Doofenshmirtz burst into the museum. "Norm! Oh, no! Norm! What did he do to you?" Dr. Doofenshmirtz howled. "Did the bad little platypus switch you off? I'll fix that!"

Dr. Doofenshmirtz ripped the ox helmet off of Norm and flipped the switch back to ON. Norm's eyes flashed as the robot came

back to life. "My name is Norm!" he said cheerfully.

"See? All you needed was a reboot!" Dr. Doofenshmirtz replied, smiling.

The evil doctor didn't hear Agent P creep up behind him. In one quick motion, the secret agent slapped a platypus helmet over Dr. Doofenshmirtz's head!

"Wait! Wait, what is this?" cried Dr. Doofenshmirtz. "What happened to all the lights?"

When Norm saw Dr. Doofenshmirtz

wearing the platypus helmet, his robotic eyes gleamed. "The enemy of the platypus is man!" Norm declared again. His strong metal fist bopped Dr. Doofenshmirtz, jamming the helmet even farther down onto his head.

"Ooof!" groaned Dr. Doofenshmirtz. "Oh, well, now it's stuck!" Then the evil doctor realized what would happen if he couldn't get that helmet off. Once Norm had located a platypus—or *thought* he had located a platypus—there would be no stopping the robot until he had destroyed it.

Even if it meant destroying his own creator in the process!

"Somebody help me!" Dr. Doofenshmirtz cried as he sprinted through the museum, with Norm chasing after him.

"Secretly, I'm very lonely!" Norm yelled as

he followed Dr. Doofenshmirtz.

Candace stomped down the stairs. She was ready to leave the Danville Museum and move on to more important business—such as busting her brothers. "Just wait until Mom finds out about this!" she shouted.

"Candace!" Phineas yelled as he and Ferb continued to run after her. "Looks like we owe you a big thanks for defeating the Minotaur. Who knew you had the power to turn men to stone!"

"That is *so* not true!" Candace shot back. "Who ever heard of something as silly as turning someone to stone?"

Candace spun around to leave—and came face-to-face with a group of stone statues. For a moment, she wondered if Phineas could be right.

"No . . . no, it can't be," she said out loud to herself.

Then another group of statues blocked her

path. They stared at her blankly.

"Ahhh! I did it again!" Candace screamed. "Don't look at me! Ahhh! I'm a monster! Make it stop!" Hysterical, Candace ran through the museum's gardens, where even more stone statues seemed to confirm her fears.

"It's okay, Ferb," Phineas finally said. "She's gone. You can look now."

But Ferb just shook his head. "No," he replied firmly. "Not taking any chances." He kept his hands over his eyes.

"Hey, look! There's Perry!" Phineas exclaimed, spotting his pet platypus again.

Phineas noticed his pet had disappeared for a few minutes!

Not even that could convince Ferb to uncover his eyes. "Still not looking," he said. He and Phineas were having way too much summertime fun to risk being turned into stone and missing out on the next adventure!

Part Two

Chapter 1

In their quiet, air-conditioned living room, Phineas and Ferb lounged around on the couch. They were completely mesmerized by an exciting TV documentary about Neanderthals. They had never learned so many amazing facts about ancient humans before.

"And now back to . . . *Neanderthal: Pride of the Paleolithic.* Neanderthals were great makers of tools, as well as skilled hunters," the documentary's host said. "It's also believed that they had a highly advanced language. For example: 'Ugh! Ugh! Ga-gahhhhh-uhhhhhh-ai-ai-ha! Yayayayayaya! Waaahhhh-oahhhh-hhh!'" he announced.

As the distinguished host demonstrated ancient Neanderthal language, he crawled around the set, acting like an overgrown chimp. Several women in the TV studio ran screaming from him!

"That's how they may have said, 'I love you,' or, 'Please take out the trash,'" the host continued, standing up straight and looking dignified once more. "But one day, the fateful ice storms came. The Neanderthals blamed each other for being ill-equipped to survive the harsh cold. Many were frozen in glaciers and may be preserved to this very day. We will return to this program after a brief word from our sponsor."

A commercial for the restaurant Sandwich Town flashed onto the screen, starring a man dancing around in a sandwich suit.

Phineas turned to Ferb. "I wonder if there's a caveman in the Danville Glacier," he said. Ferb looked back at Phineas and shrugged. Suddenly, Phineas's eyes lit up with

excitement. "Ferb! I know what we're going to do today!" he shouted.

The stepbrothers ran out of the house, jumped on their bikes, and raced down to Sandwich Town, where they each ordered their favorite sandwiches to go. A few minutes later, they were eating their lunches on the couch while they waited for the conclusion of *Neanderthal: Pride of the Paleolithic*. And that gave Phineas another idea.

"You know what else we should do today?" Phineas asked. "Go search for a caveman at the Danville Glacier!"

Ferb nodded in agreement. Exploring the glacier sounded like a pretty cool way to spend a warm summer day.

And who knew what they might find in the ice?

Meanwhile, Phineas and Ferb's sister, Candace, had her own plans for the day: her best friend, Stacy Hirano, was having a costume party! But first Candace had to figure out what to *wear* to the party. It was just a few hours away, and Candace still couldn't decide on a costume.

Candace tossed clothes, shoes, and accessories around her room as she tried on one costume after another.  "Oh, I've *got* to find the perfect outfit to wear to Stacy's costume party!" she cried. Then she spotted something. "That's it! A disco diva!"

But when Candace examined her reflection in the mirror—the navy polyester suit, platform shoes, and enormous orange wig—it just didn't seem right . . . especially since her crush, Jeremy Johnson, would be there.

"Nah," she decided, as she dove back into the closet to search for another costume. "I know! A corn dog!" she exclaimed when she saw the silly outfit.

But one look in the mirror changed Candace's mind. "Nah," she said again, frowning. Then she brightened. "I know! I'll ask Jeremy!"

Candace picked up her favorite teddy bear, which had a picture of Jeremy taped over its face. "What do *you* think about my costumes, Jeremy?" she asked.

"Gee, Candace," she replied, using a deeper voice, "I think you look beautiful in everything. Will you be my girlfriend?"

Brrrring! Brrrring!

"Oh, yes, Jeremy!" Candace squealed in her normal voice. She tried to ignore the ringing of her cell phone as she squeezed the teddy bear. "I'll be your girlfriend! What? The *prom?*"

Brrrring! Brrrring!

Candace sighed. Her daydream would have to wait. Frowning, she grabbed the phone. "What?" she snapped.

"Um, Candace?" a boy asked.

It was Jeremy! And Candace had just yelled at him! She had to act fast to fix the situation. "No, uh, just a minute please," she said in a low voice.

Then, taking a deep breath, Candace said sweetly, "Hi, Jeremy!"

"Hey, Candace," Jeremy replied. "Are you going to Stacy's party?"

"Yes," Candace answered.

"Cool! It's going to be wicked. I'm going as a caveman. I'll see you there," Jeremy said before he hung up.

"Bye, Jeremy!" Candace giggled as she hung up the phone. "Gee, it's perfect! I'll dress up like a cavewoman, and Jeremy and I will be all matchy, and it'll be like we're on a date!"

Candace skipped around her room, laughing gleefully as she searched for the perfect accessories for her cavewoman costume. She didn't even care that her room was getting supermessy. All that mattered now was putting together the most gorgeous cavewoman costume ever. She wanted to impress everyone at the party . . . especially Jeremy, the caveman of her dreams!

Downstairs in the garage, Phineas and Ferb loaded a wheelbarrow with everything they might need on their archaeological exploration of the Danville Glacier.

"Okay, let's go over our checklist," Phineas said, making sure they hadn't forgotten anything important. They had a shovel, a pickax, wooden planks, helmets . . . yep, that looked about right to Phineas.

Just then, the boys' parents walked into the garage. "Well, boys, we're off to the Center for Historically Relevant Botanical Gardens, a virtual treasure trove of tropical topiaries!" Mr. Fletcher announced.

"I'm sure it will be riveting," Mrs. Flynn replied as she got into the car. "What are you boys doing today?"

"Archaeological dig!" Phineas exclaimed.

"Okay," Mrs. Flynn said, buckling her seatbelt. "Don't touch the flower beds!"

"Wouldn't think of it," Phineas replied. "Hey, where's Perry?" he asked, looking around for his pet platypus. But then he shrugged. After all, he and Ferb had an adventure to begin!

Chapter 2

As Phineas and Ferb continued packing their gear, they didn't notice that Perry was standing against the side of the house. Perry's years of secret-agent training had taught him how to go unnoticed until the coast was clear. Then he could transform into Agent P—one of the best secret agents around! Maintaining his cover as an ordinary pet platypus was one of Agent P's most important responsibilities.

At last, Phineas and Ferb's parents were on their way to the botanical gardens; Phineas and Ferb were getting ready for their big dig; and Candace was occupied by a fashion crisis. Agent P knew that it was time to make his move. He crept over to the drainpipe against the side of the house. Then he entered the pipe and climbed all the way up to the top.

When Agent P emerged onto the roof, he was wearing his trademark secret-agent fedora—*and* a black-and-white magpie costume! He strapped on a pointy  bird's beak to complete his disguise.

Then Agent P ran quickly across a telephone wire, disrupting a flock of real magpies in the process. When he reached the telephone control box, Agent P leaped inside so that he could be transported directly to his headquarters. He arrived at the secret Platypus Cave and settled into a comfy captain's chair that faced the large-screen monitor where Major Monogram issued top secret assignments.

"Oh, there you are, Agent P," Major Monogram chuckled. "Carl! He fell for it!"

Carl Karl, the agency's intern, popped up on the monitor and laughed along with Major Monogram.

"We were just kidding about the whole magpie costume," Major Monogram said, grinning at Agent P.

The secret agent was not amused. Agent P rolled his eyes as he yanked off the beak.

"Anyway, Dr. Doofenshmirtz is up to something," Major Monogram continued. "Find out what he's up to!"

"Ooh!" Carl piped up. "Tell him to do it dressed as a rabbit!"

"Ooh!" Major Monogram said excitedly. "And Agent P, could you do it dressed as a bunny? Ha-ha-ha!"

"Good one, sir," Carl replied.

"A big *pink* bunny," Major Monogram continued.

Agent P just shook his head. He ripped off the rest of the magpie costume and left it on the chair. His mission—stopping Dr. Doofenshmirtz, no matter what—was no laughing matter!

Agent P raced across town to Doofenshmirtz Evil, Incorporated, the headquarters of the evil doctor. With a swipe of his computerized key card, Agent P opened the heavy doors to Dr. Doofenshmirtz's lab on the top floor.

Cautiously, the platypus stepped inside. He looked to the left. He looked to the right. But he didn't see Dr. Doofenshmirtz anywhere.

Whap!

A metal helmet attached to a rope plummeted from the ceiling, landing right on Agent P! He tried to remove the helmet, but it was firmly stuck to his head. Then the rope lifted Perry into the air and hung him from a moving conveyor belt that contained several

white lab coats. Agent P was right where Dr. Doofenshmirtz wanted him: trapped!

The conveyor belt jerked to a stop next to Dr. Doofenshmirtz's computer station, where the evil doctor was typing on a keyboard. "Perry the Platypus! Ooh, your persistence is insufferable! And by that, I mean completely sufferable," Dr. Doofenshmirtz announced, briefly looking up from the computer screen. "You are just in time, though, to watch me rid the Tri-State Area of one of my biggest pet peeves: people who dress as sandwiches to promote restaurants."

Dr. Doofenshmirtz grabbed a remote control so that he could begin a slide show for Agent P, to better explain his plan. One by one, images flickered across the screen: a man dressed as a turkey sandwich, a man dressed as a ham sandwich, and a man dressed as a hoagie loaded with meat and cheese.

"You see? You see what I mean?" Dr.

Doofenshmirtz asked, growing more and more irritated with each photo. "What *is* this? Are you a person or a food?"

Suddenly a photo of a man dressed in a taco suit flashed onto the screen. Despite himself, Dr. Doofenshmirtz smiled. "For some reason, I don't mind the taco guy so much. Look at his cute little hat!"

Then Dr. Doofenshmirtz got back to business. He walked across the room to a giant object that was covered with a large sheet. "Anyway, the whole thing sickens me to no end, which is why I created the Sandwich-Suit Remove-inator!" he declared.

With a flourish, Dr. Doofenshmirtz took off the sheet to reveal an enormous aircraft with a giant model of his face on one end!

"It sucks all the sandwich suits up into the air and then shreds them into teensy-weensy pieces!" Dr. Doofenshmirtz exclaimed proudly. "Today, I will fly all over the city and strip

anyone dressed as a sandwich right down to their skivvies! Ah-ha-ha-ha-ha!"

Agent P frowned. He had better come up with a plan—and fast!

Chapter 3

Back home, Candace had finally perfected her cavewoman costume. She twirled in front of the full-length mirror in her bedroom. The orange, leopard-spotted dress was perfect, but what really made the outfit amazing was the bone Candace had stuck through her high ponytail.

Just then, her cell phone rang. Candace decided to answer it in character. "Ooga-booga!" she exclaimed into the phone.

"Hi, it's Stace," replied Candace's best friend. "Do you think you could bring a sandwich platter to the party?"

"Sure," Candace replied. "Ooh, I'll bring roast beef! Jeremy eats roast beef on Phinedays and Satur-ferbs—"

Candace was suddenly distracted by the sight of Phineas and Ferb passing by her room, carrying crates of supplies for their archaeological dig. "Phineas and Ferb, you're lustin' for a bustin'!" she yelled.

"Candace!" Stacy interrupted. "Forget your brothers! Remember? *Jeremy?*"

"Right," Candace replied as a wide grin spread across her face. "Jeremy. Sandwiches. True love. Your house. Bye!"

Candace flipped the phone closed and clapped her hands over her heart. She sighed dreamily as she imagined spending the afternoon with Jeremy at Stacy's party. Whatever Phineas and Ferb were up to, they wouldn't dare interfere with her plans.

Because if they did, she would make sure they'd regret it!

At last, Phineas and Ferb had everything they could possibly need for their archaeological dig at the Danville Glacier. They walked through town pulling their red wagon—and its heavy load of tools and supplies—until they reached the icy mountain that towered over Danville.

"Well, Ferb, let's scout around and see what's what," Phineas said as the boys peered into a tunnel in the glacier. As they stepped inside, a blast of freezing air greeted them.

"All right, let's see," Phineas said thoughtfully. He and Ferb glanced around at the perfectly preserved creatures—a stegosaur, a pterodactyl, a mastodon—forever frozen in the ice. "Jurassic, Cretaceous, Pleistocene . . . oh, here's Paleolithic, down here on the end!" Phineas shouted.

The boys exchanged an excited grin as they hurried down to the Paleolithic section of the glacier. There, they found exactly what they had been looking for: a real caveman encased in ice! They grabbed their pickaxes and went right to work, chipping at the ice until a chunk of it—with the caveman still inside—cracked and fell off. Together, they hoisted the block of ice into the red wagon and carted it all the way home. As they returned to their house, Candace was so busy admiring herself in a handheld mirror that she didn't even notice her brothers pass by the living room windows.

"Ooh, oh, yeah!" Candace sang at the top of her lungs. "After Jeremy sees me lookin' so fly, he's gonna want to be my guy! Uh-huh! Uh-huh!"

Brrring!

Candace stopped singing and grabbed her phone. "Oh, hi, Stacy! Yes! Sandwiches! I'm on it!"

As Candace ran into the kitchen to make

sandwiches for the party, Phineas and Ferb pushed the wagon into the garage. Then the boys stood back to admire their very own frozen caveman.

"This will be fantastic!" Phineas exclaimed. "Think of all the practical applications a caveman can have in the modern world."

The boys plugged in a pair of yellow hair dryers and started to defrost their caveman.

"Actually, you know, besides politics, I can't think of anything," Phineas continued. "But wait until he sees what we've done with the wheel . . . with fire . . . with shiny objects!"

Finally, the glacier chunk cracked and broke apart. At last, the caveman was free!

"We did it!" Phineas cheered.

The caveman stood up. He was tall and hairy, with a shaggy brown beard. He wore a tunic made out of furry animal skins and carried a large wooden club. "Me . . . Conk,"

the caveman introduced himself, pounding on his chest.

"Me, Phineas," Phineas replied. He pointed to his stepbrother. "He, Ferb."

"Conk hungry!" Conk announced. "Food!" Conk charged across the garage and grabbed a shiny object off Mr. Fletcher's workbench.

"Oh, no, Conk! That's a carburetor!" Phineas exclaimed.

But that didn't stop Conk. He started to chew on the engine part, his yellow teeth gnashing back and forth. Bits of metal sprayed out of his mouth.

"Uh, seriously, Conk, me go to kitchen for

food while you wait here with Ferb," Phineas said quickly. "Wow! Not a very sophisticated palette," Phineas whispered to his brother.

In the kitchen, Phineas found Candace humming along as she made dozens of sandwiches for Stacy's party. "Hey, Candace!" he said cheerfully. "You think you could spare a sandwich?"

Candace was in such a good mood that she handed Phineas a sandwich right away.

"Well, I'm sure I can spare one," she said happily.

"Thanks, sis," Phineas replied. "Cool outfit, by the way. You should meet our new friend. He's a real Neanderthal."

But Candace just rolled her eyes. "Me hang out with one of *your* friends? *Puh-lease*. Now run along before I take my sandwich back.

And if you even *think* about trying something funny today, you're going to get it," she told her younger brother, giving him a serious look.

"Get what?" Phineas asked curiously.

"*It!*" Candace yelled. Then she picked up the platter of sandwiches and marched away.

"Well if '*it*' is another sandwich, I'll take it now, please!" Phineas called after her. He had a feeling that after spending thousands of years in a block of ice, Conk was going to be very hungry!

Chapter 4

Across town at the headquarters of Doofenshmirtz Evil, Incorporated, the evil doctor was just about ready to launch his latest sinister plan. While Agent P was still stuck hanging from the conveyor belt, the doctor climbed into the cockpit of the Sandwich-Suit Remove-inator. "At last!" he shouted, cackling. "My efforts have come to fruition, and nothing can stop me!"

Dr. Doofenshmirtz triumphantly pulled on the control lever. But the Sandwich-Suit Remove-inator's engine revved twice, then died. Dr. Doofenshmirtz frowned, peered at the control panel, and discovered that his latest invention was out of fuel.

With a sigh, he climbed out of the cockpit and ran across the lab to the gas pump. "I *told* Vanessa she has to fill it up," he grumbled as he filled up the fuel tank. His teenage daughter, Vanessa Doofenshmirtz, didn't always listen to what her father told her to do. He watched the price-counter carefully and shut off the pump the instant he'd pur-chased exactly eight hundred dollars of fuel. "Ahhh, yes! All zeros make it so much easier to balance my checkbook—" he began.

Then Dr. Doofenshmirtz saw something so shocking that he stopped talking in midsentence. "Perry the Platypus, are you *asleep?*" he said with a gasp.

Agent P jolted awake, but it was too late. He had been caught napping.

Dr. Doofenshmirtz sighed as he climbed back into the cockpit. What was the point of narrating an evil plan if his very own nemesis wasn't even listening?

"Where was I?" Dr. Doofenshmirtz asked, trying to get excited about his evil scheme again. "'At last' . . . well . . . you remember the rest!"

Without any more delays, Dr. Doofenshmirtz fired up the Sandwich-Suit Remove-inator. Jets of fire burst out of the aircraft's rocket boosters as Dr. Doofenshmirtz flew his invention through a hole in the wall.

His reign of terror against anyone wearing a sandwich suit was about to commence . . .

and there wasn't a single soul in the world who could stop him now!

Or . . . so he thought!

The moment Dr. Doofenshmirtz was gone, Agent P grabbed one of the lab coats near him and used its hanger to pick the helmet's lock. Instantly, the helmet released him. Now Perry

was free to sabotage Dr. Doofenshmirtz's scheme! He whistled loudly. Seconds later, Agent P's own rocket-powered jet blasted through one of the walls of Doofenshmirtz Evil, Incorporated. He

jumped into the cockpit and flew after the Sandwich-Suit Remove-inator.

Meanwhile, Dr. Doofenshmirtz cruised above the streets of Danville, looking for people dressed in sandwich suits. Outside a small restaurant called The Sammich Shop, he spotted his first victim.

"Well, well, well. What do you know?" Dr. Doofenshmirtz said. "A hapless sandwich man. Prepare to be eaten by the Remove-inator!"

Dr. Doofenshmirtz yanked on a pair of levers to start up the powerful suction of his creation.

Suddenly, the sandwich suit was sucked right into the invention, leaving the poor man wearing only his underwear! "Mother of Mayonnaise!" he cried in horror.

"Yes!" Dr. Doofenshmirtz cheered. "It's functioning properly!"

But Dr. Doofenshmirtz's glee didn't last long: Agent P was approaching! "Oh, no!" he gasped. "Perry the Platy—"

Whap!

In one swift movement, Agent P leaped into the Remove-inator, knocking over Dr. Doofenshmirtz. They battled through the aircraft, punching and kicking, until Perry reached the controls.  Before Dr. Doofenshmirtz could stop him, Agent P released the sandwich suit! It fell to the ground not far from Phineas and Ferb's house.

All of a sudden, Agent P felt a pair of hands grab him.

"I've got you now, Perry the Platy— *oof!*" Dr. Doofenshmirtz cried.

The evil doctor's triumphant exclamation was interrupted by a kick to the face! Agent P's kick was so strong, in fact, that it knocked Dr. Doofenshmirtz right over the side of the Remove-inator!

"Curse you, Perry the Platy—*ugh!*" he shouted.

Dr. Doofenshmirtz fell to the ground, and into some bushes. But Agent P couldn't stop to check on him. The Sandwich-Suit Remove-inator was about to crash into the Danville Glacier! It was too late to change course—the aircraft was just seconds away from impact. So Agent P activated his parachute and leaped overboard, escaping from the Remove-inator right before it crashed. He drifted to the ground safely.

The Danville Glacier wasn't so lucky, though. The force of the crash—and the Sandwich-Suit Remove-inator's fiery jets—shattered the glacier into millions of pieces. In moments, the towering mountain of ice that had stood over Danville for centuries was gone.

But on the bright side, there were enough ice chips for everyone in the city to enjoy a delicious snow cone on the hot summer day!

Chapter 5

In the garage, Ferb had his hands full. Conk was starving! And the garage was full of all sorts of strange and wonderful things to explore . . . and eat. But Ferb believed that he and Phineas had a responsibility to feed their caveman pal real food. So while Phineas tried to get more sandwiches, Ferb did his best to keep Conk from eating anything dangerous—such as power tools!

Then Conk found a vacuum and put it to his mouth to take a bite. But when he accidentally switched it on, the caveman sucked up his own beard! As soon as Ferb untangled Conk from the vacuum, Conk knocked a deep-sea–diver's helmet onto his head—and he had no idea how to get it off!

Fortunately, Phineas came back just in time. "Hey, guys! Good news!" he called, waving some cans of orange soda and a sandwich in the air. "I've got refreshments!"

Conk growled excitedly as he ripped off the helmet. He grabbed the sandwich and swallowed it in one gulp!

"A little something to wash it down?" Phineas asked as he offered Conk a soda. He and Ferb watched

in amazement as Conk chugged all six sodas at once!

"I guess we'd be hungry, too, if we hadn't eaten in twenty-eight thousand years," Phineas remarked. "Come on, Ferb. Let's go wrangle up some snacks for our new pal."

As Phineas and Ferb walked out of the garage, Phineas turned back to Conk and held up his hand to stop him from following them. "*You* stay put," he told Conk. Even Phineas knew that a caveman roaming the streets of Danville would not be a good thing!

But after Phineas and Ferb left, Conk was too hungry to follow Phineas's instructions . . . especially when the smell of delicious sandwiches was so tempting! Sniffing the air, Conk followed the scent outside, where Candace was carrying the giant platter of sandwiches to Stacy's house.

When Conk caught a glimpse of the sandwiches, he started to drool. "Sandwiches!" he shouted excitedly. Then he charged after Candace.

"Good news!" Phineas announced at that moment, as he and Ferb returned to the garage with a plate of sandwiches. "We've got a plethora of sandwiches for you!"

But the garage was empty.

"Um, Conk?" Phineas called out. "Uh-oh." He and Ferb ran outside to search for Conk. It was up to them to find him . . . before anyone else noticed that there was a caveman on the loose!

Candace was so excited about Stacy's party that she didn't realize Conk was following her down the street. By the time Candace knocked on Stacy's door, Conk was right

behind her—and helping himself to every sandwich she had made!

Candace couldn't ignore the chewing and chomping noises for long. She turned around to see who it was. "Jeremy, is that you?" she asked. "Wow, great costume! I hardly recognize you!"

Candace grinned happily. She thought that it was just *too* perfect that she and Jeremy had arrived at Stacy's house at the exact same time. She didn't realize that the caveman standing behind her was an *actual* caveman!

Just then, Stacy answered the door. "Yay, it's Candace!" she cried. But Stacy didn't recognize the strange figure behind her friend. "And . . ."

"And Jeremy!" Candace announced.

"And you guys are all matchy!" Stacy exclaimed as she glanced at her own Little Bo Peep costume.

"Yeah," Candace said dreamily. It was *so*

romantic to go to a party in matching outfits. Now *everyone* would know that she and Jeremy were made for each other!

"Hey, everybody!" Stacy shouted as she led Candace and Conk inside. "Candace and Jeremy are here!"

The other party guests were amazed by the guy in the very realistic caveman costume, too. As everyone stared at them, Candace shyly reached out and grabbed the caveman's hand.

"Jeremy, dude!" a guy in a robot costume said as he walked over to Conk. "Sweet costume, bro!"

Conk had never seen a robot before, and figured the shiny creature must be some sort of enemy. The caveman made a fist and socked the robot right in the face!

"Okay," the guy said quickly as he backed away. "You're not my bro!"

"Come on! Let's dance," Stacy suggested. She turned on the stereo.

"Oh, I love this song!" Candace squealed. "Dance with me, Jeremy!"

But the loud beat made Conk angry. "Rarrrrrgggggggghhhhh!" he yelled, plugging his fingers in his ears as he ran across the room. Before anyone could stop him, Conk smashed the stereo into pieces!

"Uh . . . ha-ha, ha-ha," Candace laughed nervously as Conk stomped on the broken stereo.

Then Conk saw something that made him immediately forget the loud music: the food table, loaded with all kinds of snacks and treats.

"Food!" Conk yelled as he charged over to the buffet.

As Conk emptied an entire bowl of potato chips into his mouth, Candace squeezed between him and the table.

"Hey, Jeremy! Isn't this a great party?" she asked, trying to get him to pay attention to her.

But Conk wasn't going to let anyone stand between him and the food. He lifted Candace into the air and slung her over his shoulder.

"Jeremy, you're so *primitive!*" Candace giggled.

Stacy, however, was starting to get a little worried. The person in the caveman costume wasn't acting like Jeremy at all. She hurried over to the food table. "Candace—" she began.

Brrring! Candace's cell phone suddenly rang.

"Hold that thought," Candace said to Stacy as she answered her phone. "Hello?"

"Hey, Candace," Jeremy said on the other end of the line. "Sorry I'm running late, but I just finished getting ready."

"Yeah, you look amazing!" replied Candace.

Then Jeremy's words dawned on her. If Jeremy was on the phone, then *who* was holding her over his shoulder? Her smile began to fade. "Wait—what?" she asked, confused.

"See you soon," Jeremy said. He hung up the phone.

"Who was that?" Stacy asked.

"J-j-j-j—" stammered Candace.

"Huh?" Stacy asked. "I don't know a J-j-j-j."

"But if that was . . ." Candace said, "then who . . . ?"

Just then, a memory flashed through Candace's mind. What had Phineas said to her in the kitchen? Something about "a real Neanderthal"?

Suddenly, everything made sense.

"*Ooooh!*" Candace screamed in outrage. "Phineas and Ferb are behind this!" She immediately dialed her parents. "Mom!" Candace howled into the phone.

As Mr. Fletcher drove back from the botanical gardens, Mrs. Flynn listened patiently to Candace's complaints. "Uh-huh," she said.

"So, what is it this time?" asked Mr. Fletcher after Mrs. Flynn hung up.

"She says they have a real caveman," Mrs. Flynn replied.

"Well, you can say what you like about Candace, but there's nothing *primitive* about her imagination!" joked Mr. Fletcher.

* * *

Back at the party, Candace was growing more outraged as Conk continued to stuff his face. "I demand you let me go, you . . . you . . . friend of Phineas and Ferb!" she yelled. Suddenly, Conk dropped Candace on the

floor. He had more important things to do—
like to eat more sandwiches!

"When my mom gets here, you're going to
be in *big* trouble!" Candace announced as she
got up off the floor.

Just then, Phineas and Ferb rushed up to
the door. "There you are, Conk!" Phineas
exclaimed. "Lookie, lookie!"

Ferb held up a platter of sandwiches to
tempt Conk back outside. Since Conk had
finished all the other
food at the party, he
raced over to the sand-
wiches—just as Phineas
and Ferb had hoped he
would.

"There you go, Conky," Phineas said
happily as the caveman scarfed down the
sandwiches. "There you go."

Across Stacy's yard, there was suddenly a
rustle in the bushes. Dr. Doofenshmirtz stood

up, rubbing his eyes and trying to figure out what had happened. He couldn't remember anything after Agent P had tossed him over the side of the Sandwich-Suit Remove-inator.

"Ugh," Dr. Doofenshmirtz groaned. "What smells like mustard?"

Suddenly, Dr. Doofenshmirtz looked down—and realized that he was dressed in one of the very sandwich suits he hated! He

must have fallen into it when he crashed! He gasped in horror.

At that very moment, Conk finished the last sandwich Phineas and Ferb had brought him.

He glanced across the yard, where he saw the most beautiful sight he'd ever seen: a man-size sandwich!

"There big sandwich!" Conk exclaimed in delight. He charged after Dr. Doofenshmirtz.

The evil doctor ran down the street screaming.

Phineas and Ferb watched calmly as the caveman ran off. "Well, I guess we can't compete with a sandwich like that," Phineas finally said. "They say if you love something, let it go."

"Especially if it's a caveman," Ferb added.

"Yeah," Phineas agreed, nodding his head. "*Especially* if it's a caveman!" Phineas smiled as he considered their adventures with Conk. Now *that* was pretty cool, he thought. Another awesome day of summer vacation. I wonder what's in store for us tomorrow!

Don't miss the fun in the next
Phineas & Ferb book...

Journey to Mars

Adapted by Ellie O'Ryan
Based on the series created by Dan Povenmire & Jeff "Swampy" Marsh

Phineas and Ferb's friend, Baljeet, is working on an awesome project for the summer-school science fair—he's building a giant portal to Mars! But when Phineas and Ferb's sister, Candace, accidentally goes through the portal and lands on the barren planet, will Phineas and Ferb be able to come to her rescue? Or will this turn out to be an intergalactic disaster?